Arctic Blast!

By Ace Landers
Illustrated by Dave White

SCHOLASTIC INC.

New York   Toronto   London   Auckland
Sydney   Mexico City   New Delhi   Hong Kong

ISBN 978-0-545-33455-6

12 11 10 9 8 7 6 5 4 3 2 1   12 13 14 15 16 17/0

Printed in the U.S.A.   40
First printing, January 2012

In the coldest place on Earth, there is a secret racecourse.

Welcome to the Arctic Blast! The whole racetrack is made of ice!

Only the best drivers dare to enter this race.

The racers speed down the starting ramp. There is a small hill ahead.

The small hill leads to some big air!

The purple car falls off the track.

Everyone else lands the
jump. Now the track is
starting to crack!

The cars zip around the first turn.

The red car tries to take the lead.

It crashes and breaks the track wall!
The other racers dodge the wreck.

The lead car stays in first place. Its tires are strong!

These tires are made to drive on ice. They grip the track.

The track leads the racers
up a mountain. The cars
will need their strong tires.

Watch out! The black car slips off the steep slope.

The racers reach the top. Look at the sky! It is the Northern Lights!

The colors flash and glow.
Drivers, keep your eyes on
the road!

The course heads back down the mountain.

The cars zigzag along a twisted track.

One more ramp stands between the racers and the finish line.

The first car launches into the air.

But when it lands, it shatters the track!

All of the cars fall
into an ice cave.

But no one slows down.
The racers dash up the
walls of the cave.

The cars are going too fast.
The ice cave was not made
for racing.

The cave begins to crack.
The racers dodge the falling ice.

Oh, no! A cliff is just ahead! With a burst of speed, the cars race over the edge.

Where will they land?

The green car wins the Arctic Blast!